How the
Camel got his
Hump

by Rudyard Kipling

Retold by Anna Milbourne

Illustrated by John Joven

Long ago, in the days when the world had just begun,
Camel didn't have a hump on his back as he does today.

Instead he looked like this...

This is the story, dearest reader,
of how he came to have a hump.

When the world was so new-and-all,
there was lots of work to do.

People were always busy hammering and chopping and fetching and carrying. Horse, Dog and Ox helped.

But Camel was as lazy as the day was long.
He didn't work. He just stood around, chomping
on leaves and enjoying the sunshine.

Not only that, but
he was grumpy too.

"Please can you help me fetch sticks?" Dog asked Camel.

"HUMPH!" Camel snorted rudely, and carried right on eating.

"Please can you help
me bring branches?"
asked Horse.

Camel snorted again. Then he stood there with his
nose in the air until Horse gave up and trudged away.

"Please will you help me pull this heavy cart?" asked Ox. "It would be easier with two of us."

Camel shook his head.
"HUMPH!" was his only reply.

The animals went to complain to Man.
"It's not fair," they moaned. "Camel won't help."

Man shrugged. "If Camel won't help,
you three will just have to work harder."

The animals looked at Camel,
lazing around doing nothing.

And they felt really,
really cross.

Just then, a desert storm blew up... Out of the whirling, swirling sand, came a magic genie.

The animals rushed up to him, hoping he could help. "Camel does nothing but eat and sleep, while we do all the work," they told him. "We wish he'd change!"

"Your wish is my command," said the genie.

So the genie went to find Camel.
"What's all this I hear about you
not working?" he asked.

Can you guess what Camel replied? "HUMPH!"
"The others have to work harder because
you're so lazy," the genie added.

"HUMPH!" said Camel again.

"Don't say that too often, or you might regret it," the genie warned. "This is your last chance, Camel. Will you do some work?"

"HUMPH!"

said Camel, and carried on munching.

The genie waved his arms.
There was a zap...whoosh...
...FLASH...

...and a big, hairy hump sprouted on Camel's back!

"WHAT'S THAT?"
he gasped.

"Your HUMPH!"
the genie chuckled.
"It will help you work."

"How can that thing help me?" asked Camel.

The genie laughed. "Your humph stores
food so you won't have to eat so often."

"You can catch up on your work
while everyone else stops for lunch!"

Ever since that day, Camel has worked hard.
He still has his 'humph' on his back.

(Although nowadays people
call it a 'hump', so as not
to hurt his feelings.)

But he is as grumpy and bad-mannered as ever.

HUMPH!

'How the Camel got his Hump' is from the book
'Just So Stories' by Rudyard Kipling, which tells stories
of how animals came to be the way they are.

Edited by Lesley Sims
Designed by Laura Nelson Norris

First published in 2018 by Usborne Publishing Ltd., Usborne House, 83-85 Saffron Hill,
London EC1N 8RT, England. www.usborne.com Copyright © 2018, 2017 Usborne Publishing Ltd.